Disney
Winnie the Pooh

It's Fun to Learn

Playing Pirates

On a sunny autumn afternoon, Tigger was trying hard to think of a fun activity. "Today is a great day for something fun," he said. "But what could that something be?"

"I know who'll know!" he exclaimed. And with that, he bounced out the door and down the path through the Hundred-Acre Wood. He was headed for Christopher Robin's house.

On the way, Tigger noticed something stuck to a tree. "What's this?" he wondered, bouncing up to get a better look. It was a piece of paper with some strange drawings on it and a big "X" right in the middle.

"Hoo-hoo-hoo! X marks the spot!" he exclaimed. He grabbed the piece of paper and rushed off to tell his friends.

Pooh, Piglet, and Roo were about to have a little snack when Tigger came
bouncing in with the piece of paper.

"Look what I found!" he said.

"What is it?" asked Roo.

"It's a pirates' treasure map, of course!" said Tigger.

"P-p-p-pirates?" said Piglet. "I don't think I like pirates…"

"Hmmm," thought Pooh, licking the sticky honey off his fingers. "I suppose Tigger could be right."

So they took the map to Christopher Robin.

Christopher Robin looked it over carefully. "If we follow the clues," he said thoughtfully, "we'll find where the great pirate treasure is buried."

"Well, what are we waiting for?" shouted Tigger. "Let's get goin'!"

"I've always wanted to find buried treasure," said Roo.

But first, the friends needed to dress up pretending to be pirates for their Pirate Treasure Hunt. Christopher Robin brought out his toy chest and began looking through it.

"Try this," said Christopher Robin, placing a pirate hat on Piglet's head.

"Ahoy, there!" shouted Tigger, looking through his telescope.

Pooh was in charge of reading the map. "I think we go that-a-way," he said, pointing out the door. "Then this-a-way…or maybe the other way. Oh, bother…."

They sailed down the stream aboard their make-believe pirate ship, which they named *The Pooh Bear*.

"Keep your eyes open for treasure, mateys," commanded Captain Christopher Robin.

"Aye-aye, captain!" said First Mate Tigger. "But I don't see anything but a bunch of trees and rocks."

"Look harder," replied Christopher Robin. "Use your imagination, Tigger."

Just then, Roo spotted something. "Captain!" he squealed. "I see gold!"

As they dug for treasure they made up a silly pirate song:

Yo-ho-ho and diddly-dum-dee-dee,

There'll be treasure for you and treasure for me!

"Wow!" said Roo. "Wait till Mama sees what we found!"

"One, two, three, four, five pieces of gold," counted Piglet. "That's one for each of us."

"But there must be even BIGGER treasure buried somewhere else," said Tigger. "Where do we go next?"

Pooh studied the map. "Hmmm," he said, scratching his head. "It appears to be buried under a mountain."

"Where are we going to find a mountain?" asked Piglet.

Tigger spied something through his telescope in the distance. "Mountain, ahoy!" he shouted and bounced off.

"Shhh!" whispered Captain Christopher Robin. "There are bandits guarding the treasure."

"Let me at 'em!" said Roo, waving his sword.

"No, we'll have to sneak up and surprise them," said Tigger.

So they came up with a plan.

Little Roo manned the cannon. Pooh and Christopher Robin readied the net.
Piglet was a little nervous, but volunteered to stand guard.

"Is the secret weapon ready?" asked Captain Christopher Robin.

"Ready!" called Tigger. He pretended to stand on the plank of the pirate ship, prepared to pounce on the bandits.

"Ready, aim, fire!" yelled Christopher Robin.

With that, the mighty crew of *The Pooh Bear* launched the cannon...and their secret weapon—First Mate Tigger.

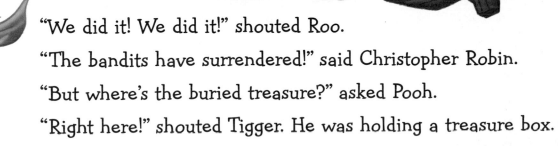

"We did it! We did it!" shouted Roo.

"The bandits have surrendered!" said Christopher Robin.

"But where's the buried treasure?" asked Pooh.

"Right here!" shouted Tigger. He was holding a treasure box.

"Open it, Tigger!" cried Roo.

"Maybe there's more gold inside," said Piglet.

"Or some golden honey," suggested Pooh.

"Nope," said Tigger, peeking under the lid.

It was much better than that! Inside was an invitation to Christopher Robin's birthday celebration!

"Yo-ho-ho! Now everyone can come to my pirate party!" said Christopher Robin.

At the party, Tigger was busily digging into a big ice-cream sundae.

"Now that was a Tigger-riffic day!" he said.

"And all you had to do was make believe and use your imagination," said Christopher Robin.

"Can I make believe it's tomorrow?" asked Tigger.

"Why?" asked a puzzled Pooh. He was quite happy having a smackerel of honey with his cake.

"So we can use our imaginations and go on a whole new adventure again," Tigger replied. "I just can't wait!"

Fun to Learn Activity

Ahoy there, mateys! X marked the spot for our tiggerific game of pirates! Can you go back through the story and find all the real things we used for our pretend pirate stuff?

Use your imagination to make up your own story and act it out with your friends!